This book belongs to ...

Melissa and Jeremy.

©Illus. Dr. Seuss 1957

For more information about The Beginning Readers Program
featuring books by Dr. Seuss & His Friends:
Call **1-800-955-9877**
Or Write: Grolier Direct Marketing
Sherman Turnpike, Danbury, CT 06816

GROLIER
BOOK CLUB EDITION

The FOOT BOOK

Dear Parent,

I am delighted to send you this FREE book, and to help introduce your child to the joys that only reading can bring.

You see, some books are read and forgotten. But Beginner Books by Dr. Seuss are timeless classics that have delighted children for generations.

That's right. Dr. Seuss is one of the all-time greatest *and* best-loved children's writers. And for good reason: his stories feature such ingenious characters, wondrous images and imaginative language, they can't help but thrill, entertain *and* instruct.

Just open your FREE book and see for yourself. Watch as your child points to the big feet, the pig feet, his or her own left and right feet. Why, already, the learning has begun!

And, because *The Foot Book* is one of the earliest learning books in the program, that's just the beginning. As you'll soon see, Dr. Seuss and His Friends will continue to charm your child with stories he or she will *never* outgrow!

I'm sure you and your child will enjoy this FREE book ... again and again and again.

Sincerely,

Barbara Gregory

Barbara Gregory
Editor-in-Chief
Grolier Direct Marketing

Families Grow With Products From Grolier.

The
FOOT
BOOK

By
Dr. Seuss

A Bright & Early Book

RANDOM HOUSE / NEW YORK

X Y Z

Left foot
Left foot

Right foot
Right

Feet in the morning

Feet at night

Left foot

Left foot

Left foot

Right

Wet foot

Dry foot

High foot

Low foot

Front feet

Back feet

Red feet

Black feet

Left foot   Right foot

Feet   Feet   Feet

How many, many
feet you meet.

Slow feet

Quick feet

Trick feet

Sick feet

Up feet

Down feet

Here come clown feet.

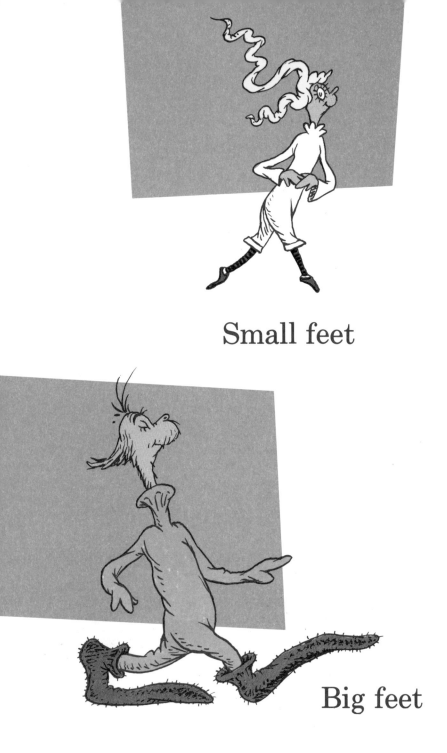

Small feet

Big feet

Here come pig feet.

His feet

Her feet

Fuzzy fur feet

In the house,
and on the street,

how many, many
feet you meet.

Up in the air feet

Over a chair feet

More and more feet

Twenty-four feet

Here come
more and more . . . .

.... and more feet!

Left foot.   Right foot.

Feet. Feet. Feet.

Oh, how many
feet you meet!